W9-BSK-666

It's Winter, Dear Dragon

by Margaret Hillert
Illustrated by David Schimmell

NORWOOD HOUSE PRESS

DEAR CAREGIVER, The *Beginning-to-Read* series is a carefully written collection of classic readers you may remember from your own childhood. Each book features text comprised of common sight words to provide your child ample practice reading the words that appear most frequently in written text. The many additional details in the pictures enhance the story and offer the opportunity for you to help your child expand oral language and develop comprehension.

Begin by reading the story to your child, followed by letting him or her read familiar words and soon your child will be able to read the story independently. At each step of the way, be sure to praise your reader's efforts to build his or her confidence as an independent reader. Discuss the pictures and encourage your child to make connections between the story and his or her own life. At the end of the story, you will find reading activities and a word list that will help your child practice and strengthen beginning reading skills.

Above all, the most important part of the reading experience is to have fun and enjoy it!

Shannon Cannon

Shannon Cannon,
Literacy Consultant

Norwood House Press • P.O. Box 316598 • Chicago, Illinois 60631
For more information about Norwood House Press please visit our website at *www.norwoodhousepress.com* or call 866-565-2900.

LIBRARY OF CONGRESS CATALOGING-IN-PUBLICATION DATA
    Hillert, Margaret.
     It's winter, dear Dragon / by Margaret Hillert ; illustrated by David Schimmell.
       p. cm. — (A beginning-to-read book)
     Summary: "A boy and his pet dragon go sledding, make a snow fort, and have a snowball fight with friends on a fun winter day"—Provided by publisher.
     ISBN-13: 978-1-59953-314-8 (lib. ed. : alk. paper)
     ISBN-10: 1-59953-314-6 (lib. ed. : alk. paper) [1. Dragons--Fiction. 2. Winter--Fiction.] I. Schimmell, David, ill. II. Title. III. Title: It is winter, dear Dragon.
    PZ7.H558Iuw 2009
    [E]--dc22
                 2009003890
Manufactured in the United States of America in North Mankato, Minnesota.
167R—112010

Look here.
Look at the snow!
We can go out
and play in it.

Yes, yes.
You can go out but
put this on
        and this
        and this.

Oh, how pretty.
See how pretty the snow is.

I can make a big ball of snow.
You can help me.
Do this.
Make a big one.

Now—
I will put this one
up on this one.

And I will do something funny.
Look at this—
      and this.

Now do this.
See what we can make.

One looks like me.
One looks like you.

Oh, look.
I see some friends.
Friends are fun to play with.
We will have fun now!

We have to go up—
and up—
and up.

Then we come down—
down, down, down, down, down.

We will make a big snow house.
It will be a help to us.

Now—
Look out!
Look out!
Here it comes.

I got you!
I got you!

That was fun, but
I have to go now.

Mother. Mother.
Do you have something for me?
Something to eat?

Come in.
Come in.
I do have something for you.

O-O-O-Oh! Cookies!
Good cookies.
I will eat one—
	and two—
		and three.

Oh, Father.
Look at this book.
Can you help me with this?

Yes, yes.
Let me see this.
It is a good one.

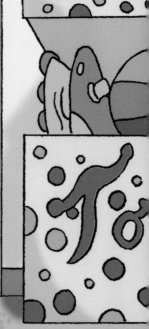

That was good.
Now I will put it away.
I will put all this away.

27

Here you are with me.
And here I am with you.
Oh, how good it is to be
with you, dear dragon.

The following activities support the findings of the National Reading Panel that determined the most effective components for reading instruction are: Phonemic Awareness, Phonics, Vocabulary, Fluency, and Text Comprehension.

Phonemic Awareness: The /sn/ consonant blend

Sound Substitution: Say the word parts on the right to your child. Ask your child to repeat the word part, adding the /sn/ sound to the beginning to make a word:

sn + ow = snow	sn + ag = snag	sn + iff = sniff
sn + ug = snug	sn + out = snout	sn + ack = snack
sn + ail = snail	sn + ap = snap	sn + eeze = sneeze
sn + ake = snake		

Phonics: The sn- consonant cluster

1. Demonstrate how to form the letters **sn** for your child.

2. Have your child practice writing **sn** at least three times.

3. Divide a piece of paper in half by folding it the long way. Draw a line on the fold. Turn it so that the paper has two columns. Write the word parts above in the left column.

4. Ask your child to make the new words in the right column by adding **sn** in front of the word parts.

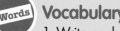

Vocabulary: Verb Tenses

1. Write each of the following words on separate index cards:

snow/snowing/snowed   build/building/built
make/making/made   eat/eating/ate
look/looking/looked   play/playing/played

go/going/gone
help/helping/helped
climb/climbing/climbed

read/reading/read
come/coming/came
do/doing/done

2. Mix up the index cards and ask your child to group them in verb families. Ask your child to place the verbs in each family according to tense (present, present + ing, past) and read them aloud in order.

3. Put the cards in a paper bag and shake it to mix them up. Take turns selecting cards from the bag and stating sentences using the words.

Fluency: Shared Reading

1. Reread the story to your child at least two more times while your child tracks the print by running a finger under the words as they are read. Ask your child to read the words he or she knows with you.

2. Reread the story taking turns, alternating readers between sentences or pages.

Text Comprehension: Discussion Time

1. Ask your child to retell the sequence of events in the story.

2. To check comprehension, ask your child the following questions:
   - What did the mother have the boy and dear dragon put on before going out? Why?
   - Name three things the boy made with the snow? (snowman, snow angels, snow house)
   - What did the boy do with his father?
   - What do you like to do in winter? Why?

WORD LIST

It's Winter, Dear Dragon uses the 72 words listed below.
This list can be used to practice reading the words that appear in the text.
You may wish to write the words on index cards and use them to help your
child build automatic word recognition. Regular practice with these words
will enhance your child's fluency in reading connected text.

a	do	house	oh	to
all	down	how	on	two
am	dragon		one	
and		I	out	up
are	eat	in		us
at		is	play	
away	Father	it	pretty	was
	for		put	we
ball	friends	let		what
be	fun	like	see	will
big	funny	look(s)	snow	with
book			some	
but	go	make	something	yes
	good	me		you
can	got	Mother	that	
come(s)			the	
cookies	have	now	then	
	help		this	
dear	here	of	three	

ABOUT THE AUTHOR Margaret Hillert has written over 80 books for
children who are just learning to read. Her books
have been translated into many different languages and over a million children
throughout the world have read her books. She first started writing poetry as
a child and has continued to write for children and adults throughout her life. A
first grade teacher for 34 years, Margaret is now retired from teaching and lives in
Michigan where she likes to write, take walks in the morning, and care for her three cats.

Photograph by Glenna Washburn

ABOUT THE ADVISER Shannon Cannon contributed the activities pages that appear in
this book. Shannon serves as a literacy consultant and provides
staff development to help improve reading instruction. She is a frequent presenter at educational
conferences and workshops. Prior to this she worked as an elementary school teacher and as
president of a curriculum publishing company.